It's All About
Calvin

Book 1—Lost Pup

PAMELA DAMRON

Trilogy Christian Publishers
A Wholly Owned Subsidary of Trinity Broadcasting Network
2442 Michelle Drive
Tustin, CA 92780

For information, address Trilogy Christian Publishing
Rights Department, 2442 Michelle Drive, Tustin, Ca 92780.
Trilogy Christian Publishing/ TBN and colophon are trademarks of Trinity Broadcasting Network.

For information about special discounts for bulk purchases, please contact Trilogy Christian Publishing.

Manufactured in the United States of America

10 9 8 7 6 5 4 3 2 1

Library of Congress Cataloging-in-Publication Data is available.

ISBN 978-1-64773-614-9 (Print Book)
ISBN 978-1-64773-615-6 (ebook)

To my husband, Greg, who has encouraged me to

write our entire thirty-five years together,

and our daughter, Natalee, who inspires me every day

by her wisdom and wit.

And of course, Calvin, who has turned into the best

little buddy we ever thought he could be, because, after all,

he is a beagle.

There he sat, wagging his tail,
　　Wondering when to make his move.
Such a cute little pup with big floppy ears,
　　He strutted on down with his groove.

He couldn't cross that busy street.
  What was a beagle to do?
He missed his friends, his paws felt the heat;
  Where was he? He had not a clue.

There were so many cars along the trail,
  A trail that had absolutely no end.
Aha, a nice, shady bush to take a break—
  He curled up and dreamt of friends.

"Shoo, shoo," he heard a man say;
    A big man chased him away.
Poor little beagle, with the sun beaming down;
    He was having such a rotten day!

He was hot and thirsty and getting quite tired.
    And a meal would be nice as well.
July in St. Peters is a miserable heat,
    And he'd been lost for quite a spell.

When the sun went down and
the moon lit the sky,
    The pup found a bench at a park.
He heard a sweet girl's voice coming up;
    He gave a quick bay, that fun beagle bark.

"Hello, hello," he was trying to say.
    And the girl gave him lots of hugs.
She gave him some water and a bite of her food,
    And then they came—the bugs.

The girl screamed, and off she ran;
     Into the car she jumped.
She left him there just watching her go.
     He felt once again dumped.

This little dog had a pretty good life.
     How did he get in this mess?
He was scared he was getting farther away
     From a life with so little stress.

9

This beagle had lots of brothers and sisters;
    They loved to romp and play.
Their human took them on lots of hunts.
    And then there was a dreadful day.

A day in the woods started off just great,
    Ten beagle dogs in a truck.
In the woods they scattered to each find a bunny,
    And wouldn't you know, he got stuck.

He saw a bunny and enjoyed the chase;
    Into a tree trunk he ran.
The bunny got out, he heard his human whistle,
    And he knew he would need a quick plan.

But it wasn't to be, and off the truck went,
        Leaving him alone in the woods.
He freed himself finally and he wanted his home,
        But he wasn't even close to his hood.

Why did his human leave him behind?
        "Didn't he know I'm missin'?"
He guessed his human finding all of his dogs
        Was just a beagle wishin'.

So here he was, feeling very alone,
        In the park with nothing but darkness.
There were lots of strange sounds far in the distance,
        And this pup having feelings of pure loneliness.

And then it happened, his nose in the air—
    There was a bunny or something nearby.
He didn't use his brain, his nose led the way,
    Finding that bunny, well, he had to try!

As fun as the chase happened to be,
    The beagle was hungry and tired.
His nose led him back to the park with the girl.
    How wild animals survived, he was inspired.

When he was chasing it felt like old times;
    He didn't miss his home or other pups.
But reality was, he was by himself,
    So tomorrow he would seek a new dump.

Through the night there were sounds in the woods nearby
    And a big empty field that was quiet.
The beautiful deer came out at night
    And gave him a look as they grazed a corn diet.

As the sun started to rise high above,
    He stretched a big stretch he was proud of.
He needed a drink, and a meal would be nice;
    He missed his human and all that love.

He wandered out from beyond the pavilion
    As the work trucks were moving in.
One backed up as he noticed the lone dog.
    A nice man put out water, food, and a pen.

The beagle entered the pen
    And ate what was laid out before him.
The human told him, "You're a good boy,"
    And life no longer seemed so grim.

He was taken to a shelter with more dogs and cats.
    The ladies there kissed him all over.
This wasn't going to be bad at all—
    Food and water, crate and cover.

They bathed him and fed him and treated
    Him like he was needing compassion.
One girl was rubbing his big floppy ears
    And decided his name should be Calvin.

The humans he had taking care of him
    Put him in a crate day and night.
One day he woke with a cone on his head,
    And ouch, he hurt with all his might.

Calvin made a few friends as the days went by;
    The other dogs cried in their pens.
People came and checked out each dog—
    Going home with someone was a big win.

With the pain from having something removed,
    But the cone still on his head,
He got the okay to be adopted out.
    Was he losing this big comfy bed?

And then it happened, he knew from the start,
     A family walked up to say "Hi."
The girl at the shelter said they'd love him so—
     He was such a good li'l guy.

They took him to a private playroom,
     With the cone on his head and all.
He didn't get cozy but ran after toys—
     His bay could be heard up the halls!

The woman mentioned she'd prayed for weeks
     To find a sweet dog for their bunch.
This little guy was quite active and quick,
     But she had a very calming hunch.

The gentleman patted him and said,
     "This is the dog for us.
He'll make a good addition to our family."
     His wife and daughter cooed and made such a fuss.

Yes, Calvin had found a new family indeed
     After living the past month on the run.
Their other dog that was mighty big
     Just wanted to romp and have fun.

Calvin rounded up the family to six,
     With three humans and fur babies to boot.
The retriever and the cat were laid-back and quiet;
     Calvin was loud but oh-so cute.

He took some getting used to for all in the house,
    But they loved him with all of their hearts.
No more having to find a safe place to sleep;
    He would stay till death they would part.

So Calvin, it seems, is a very lucky beagle;
    He got a second chance with his life.
No more hunting on the run for this dog,
    No more wondering or strife.

Calvin was happy to be home at last,
    A new home that passed every test.
He gets lots of hugs and kisses and treats,
    And he knows he has the very best.

So if you want a dog like Calvin
    That will make you laugh every day,
Go to your local pet adoption center.
    Enjoy the journey coming your way.

There is nothing like a pup or a kitty
    That is lonely and living in a cage.
They seem to understand the
chance you give them,
    No matter what the pet's age.

There may be some trials getting acquainted,
    But there is nothing like unconditional love.
These pets will be your best friend indeed;
    You'll be blessed from our Lord above.

    We're so happy we did! We love our Calvin!